PENGUIN AUDIOBOOKS

PENGUIN ENGLISH VERSE: VOLUME 6
THE EARLY TWENTIETH CENTURY
HARDY TO OWEN

SELECTED AND INTRODUCED
BY PAUL DRIVER

Printed in England by Clays Ltd, St Ives plc

The publishers are grateful for permission to quote from the following authors:

W. B. Yeats: to A. P. Watt Ltd on behalf of Ann Yeats and Michael Yeats. Thomas Hardy: to Macmillan Ltd. A. E. Housman: to the Society of Authors as the literary representatives of the Estate of A. E. Housman. G. K. Chesterton: to A. P. Watt Ltd on behalf of the Royal Literary Fund. D. H. Lawrence: to Laurence Pollinger Ltd and the Estate of Frieda Lawrence Ravagli. John Masefield: to the Society of Authors as the literary representatives of the Estate of John Masefield. Edward Thomas: to Myfanwy Thomas. Oliver St John Gogarty: to Oliver D. Gogarty. Edmund Blunden: to the Peters Fraser & Dunlop Group Ltd. Siegfried Sassoon: to George Sassoon.

CONTENTS

Introduction

This Audiobook comprises some of the best 'talk' in the English language. W. H. Auden's well-known definition of poetry as 'memorable speech' applies with particular justice to a survey of the tradition of English verse that is spoken end to end, as for the many hours of this series of Penguin English Verse. Of course, it is debatable just where the book-ends of this great tradition should be placed. We begin with a famous medieval lyric and end with poems by men whose perception was instructed by the First World War. But the medieval period, with its considerable linguistic difficulties for the modern reader–listener, has been mostly excluded, and the first volume of the series features the sixteenth century.

The volume divisions should not be too controversial. The poetry of John Donne is placed as a bridge between the sixteenth and seventeenth centuries; that of Dryden nicely links the seventeenth and the eighteenth. The remaining three surveys are designated not by precise date but by sensibility. *The Romantics* starts with William Blake, the poet in whom so much dammed-up emotion of eighteenth-century verse abruptly flooded free. *The Victorians* hears a new diction – both plusher and more enamelled than that of the Romantics – in a poem like Thomas Lovell Beddoes's 'A Crocodile' and proceeds as far as the work of Robert Bridges and Robert Louis Stevenson. *The*

Early Twentieth Century is announced by W. B. Yeats and Thomas Hardy, and while many of its products remain wedded to tradition, there are new notes of style and diction being sounded all the time, as in the vernacular virtuosity of Rudyard Kipling's work, the insinuating effectiveness of D. H. Lawrence or the subtle domestic psychology of lines by Edward Thomas.

Only British and Irish poets are included here. Very long poems have been ruled out, though excerpts are sometimes given. There is no *Faerie Queene* or *Paradise Lost*, but for all that the mountains of English poetry have been avoided, what unfolds in their stead is certainly no dull and level terrain. Rather it is a fabulously luxuriant profusion of genres, forms, styles and textures, both demotic and exalted, light-hearted and sublime; and our aim has been to represent this diversity as fully as possible. The ordering on each cassette-side is not chronological – criteria of rhythmic balance and tonal contrast have prevailed over the promptings of scholarship. This is an anthology for the ear, a drama of voices in which nonsense verse, jingles, 'sound poems' (like Southey's 'The Cataract of Lodore') and dialect pieces readily find their role. Through the deployment of different reading voices an attempt, however humble, has been made to orchestrate that tremendous unfolding, the history of English poetry.

Paul Driver
May 1995

He Wishes for the Cloths of Heaven

Had I the heavens' embroidered cloths,
Enwrought with golden and silver light,
The blue and the dim and the dark cloths
Of night and light and the half-light,

I would spread the cloths under your feet:
But I, being poor, have only my dreams;
I have spread my dreams under your feet;
Tread softly because you tread on my dreams.

WILLIAM BUTLER YEATS

The Lake Isle of Innisfree

I will arise and go now, and go to Innisfree,
And a small cabin build there, of clay and wattles made:
Nine bean-rows will I have there, a hive for the honey-bee,
And live alone in the bee-loud glade.

And I shall have some peace there, for peace comes
   dropping slow,
Dropping from the veils of the morning to where the
   cricket sings;
There midnight's all a glimmer, and noon a purple glow,
And evening full of the linnet's wings.

I will arise and go now, for always night and day
I hear lake water lapping with low sounds by the shore;

While I stand on the roadway, or on the pavements grey,
I hear it in the deep heart's core.

WILLIAM BUTLER YEATS

Donal Og

It is late last night the dog was speaking of you;
the snipe was speaking of you in her deep marsh.
It is you are the lonely bird through the woods;
and that you may be without a mate until you find me.

You promised me, and you said a lie to me,
that you would be before me where the sheep are flocked;
I gave a whistle and three hundred cries to you,
and I found nothing there but a bleating lamb.

You promised me a thing that was hard for you,
a ship of gold under a silver mast;
twelve towns with a market in all of them,
and a fine white court by the side of the sea.

You promised me a thing that is not possible,
that you would give me gloves of the skin of a fish;
that you would give me shoes of the skin of a bird;
and a suit of the dearest silk in Ireland.

When I go by myself to the Well of Loneliness,
I sit down and I go through my trouble;
when I see the world and do not see my boy,
he that has an amber shade in his hair.

It was on that Sunday I gave my love to you;
the Sunday that is last before Easter Sunday.
And myself on my knees reading the Passion;
and my two eyes giving love to you for ever.

My mother said to me not to be talking with you today,
or tomorrow, or on the Sunday;
it was a bad time she took for telling me that;
it was shutting the door after the house was robbed.

My heart is as black as the blackness of the sloe,
or as the black coal that is on the smith's forge;
or as the sole of a shoe left in white halls;
it was you put that darkness over my life.

You have taken the east from me; you have taken the west
    from me;
you have taken what is before me and what is behind me;
you have taken the moon, you have taken the sun from me;
and my fear is great that you have taken God from me!

ANON.

From the Irish (trans. Lady Augusta Gregory)

Neutral Tones

We stood by a pond that winter day,
And the sun was white, as though chidden of God,
And a few leaves lay on the starving sod;
    – They had fallen from an ash, and were gray.

Your eyes on me were as eyes that rove
Over tedious riddles of years ago;

And some words played between us to and fro
  On which lost the more by our love.

The smile on your mouth was the deadest thing
Alive enough to have strength to die;
And a grin of bitterness swept thereby
  Like an ominous bird a-wing . . .

Since then, keen lessons that love deceives,
And wrings with wrong, have shaped to me
Your face, and the God-curst sun, and a tree,
  And a pond edged with grayish leaves.

THOMAS HARDY

The Sorrow of Love

The quarrel of the sparrows in the eaves,
  The full round moon and the star-laden sky,
And the loud song of the ever-singing leaves
  Had hid away earth's old and weary cry.

And then you came with those red mournful lips,
  And with you came the whole of the world's tears,
And all the sorrows of her labouring ships,
  And all burden of her myriad years.

And now the sparrows warring in the eaves,
  The crumbling moon, the white stars in the sky,
And the loud chanting of the unquiet leaves,
  Are shaken with earth's old and weary cry.

WILLIAM BUTLER YEATS

Out in the Dark

Out in the dark over the snow
The fallow fawns invisible go
With the fallow doe;
And the winds blow
Fast as the stars are slow.

Stealthily the dark haunts round
And, when the lamp goes, without sound
At a swifter bound
Than the swiftest hound,
Arrives, and all else is drowned;

And star and I and wind and deer,
Are in the dark together, – near,
Yet far, – and fear
Drums on my ear
In that sage company drear.

How weak and little is the light,
All the universe of sight,
Love and delight,
Before the might,
If you love it not, of night.

EDWARD THOMAS

5

Thoughts of Phena

Not a line of her writing have I,
  Not a thread of her hair,
No mark of her late time as dame in her dwelling, whereby
  I may picture her there;
  And in vain do I urge my unsight
  To conceive my lost prize
At her close, whom I knew when her dreams were
      upbrimming with light,
  And with laughter her eyes.

What scenes spread around her last days,
  Sad, shining, or dim?
Did her gifts and compassions enray and enarch her sweet
    ways
  With an aureate nimb?
  Or did life-light decline from her years,
  And mischances control
Her full day-star; unease, or regret, or forebodings, or fears
  Disennoble her soul?

Thus I do but the phantom retain
  Of the maiden of yore
As my relic; yet haply the best of her – fined in my brain
  It may be the more
  That no line of her writing have I,
  Nor a thread of her hair,

6

No mark of her late time as dame in her dwelling, whereby
 I may picture her there.

THOMAS HARDY

'When you are old'

When you are old and grey and full of sleep,
And nodding by the fire, take down this book,
And slowly read, and dream of the soft look
Your eyes had once, and of their shadows deep;

How many loved your moments of glad grace,
And loved your beauty with love false or true,
But one man loved the pilgrim soul in you,
And loved the sorrows of your changing face;

And bending down beside the glowing bars,
Murmur, a little sadly, how Love fled
And paced upon the mountains overhead
And hid his face amid a crowd of stars.

WILLIAM BUTLER YEATS

A Broken Appointment

You did not come,
And marching Time drew on, and wore me numb. –
Yet less for loss of your dear presence there
Than that I thus found lacking in your make
That high compassion which can overbear

Reluctance for pure lovingkindness' sake
Grieved I, when, as the hope-hour stroked its sum,
      You did not come.

      You love not me,
And love alone can lend you loyalty;
– I know and knew it. But, unto the store
Of human deeds divine in all but name,
Was it not worth a little hour or more
To add yet this: Once you, a woman, came
To soothe a time-torn man; even though it be
      You love not me?

THOMAS HARDY

No Second Troy

Why should I blame her that she filled my days
With misery, or that she would of late
Have taught to ignorant men most violent ways,
Or hurled the little streets upon the great,
Had they but courage equal to desire?
What could have made her peaceful with a mind
That nobleness made simple as a fire,
With beauty like a tightened bow, a kind
That is not natural in an age like this,
Being high and solitary and most stern?
Why, what could she have done, being what she is?
Was there another Troy for her to burn?

WILLIAM BUTLER YEATS

The Self-unseeing

Here is the ancient floor,
Footworn and hollowed and thin,
Here was the former door
Where the dead feet walked in.

She sat here in her chair,
Smiling into the fire;
He who played stood there,
Bowing it higher and higher.

Childlike, I danced in a dream;
Blessings emblazoned that day;   *10*
Everything glowed with a gleam;
Yet we were looking away!

THOMAS HARDY

Brown Penny

I whispered, 'I am too young,'
And then, 'I am old enough';
Wherefore I threw a penny
To find out if I might love.
'Go and love, go and love, young man,
If the lady be young and fair.'
Ah, penny, brown penny, brown penny,
I am looped in the loops of her hair.

O love is the crooked thing,
There is nobody wise enough
To find out all that is in it,
For he would be thinking of love
Till the stars had run away
And the shadows eaten the moon.
Ah, penny, brown penny, brown penny,
One cannot begin it too soon.

Digging

To-day I think
Only with scents, – scents dead leaves yield,
And bracken, and wild carrot's seed,
And the square mustard field;

Odours that rise
When the spade wounds the root of tree,
Rose, currant, raspberry, or goutweed,
Rhubarb or celery;

The smoke's smell, too,
Flowing from where a bonfire burns
The dead, the waste, the dangerous,
And all to sweetness turns.

It is enough
To smell, to crumble the dark earth,

While the robin sings over again
Sad songs of Autumn mirth.

EDWARD THOMAS

During Wind and Rain

They sing their dearest songs –
He, she, all of them – yea,
Treble and tenor and bass,
    And one to play;
With the candles mooning each face . . .
    Ah, no; the years O!
How the sick leaves reel down in throngs!

They clear the creeping moss –
Elders and juniors – aye,
Making the pathways neat
    And the garden gay;
And they build a shady seat . . .
    Ah, no; the years, the years;
See, the white storm-birds wing across!

They are blithely breakfasting all –
Men and maidens – yea,
Under the summer tree,
    With a glimpse of the bay,
While pet fowl come to the knee . . .
    Ah, no; the years O!
And the rotten rose is ript from the wall.

10

20

11

They change to a high new house,
He, she, all of them – aye,
Clocks and carpets and chairs
    On the lawn all day,
And brightest things that are theirs . . .
    Ah, no; the years, the years;
Down their carved names the rain-drop ploughs.

THOMAS HARDY

Aspens

All day and night, save winter, every weather,
Above the inn, the smithy, and the shop,
The aspens at the cross-roads talk together
Of rain, until their last leaves fall from the top.

Out of the blacksmith's cavern comes the ringing
Of hammer, shoe, and anvil; out of the inn
The clink, the hum, the roar, the random singing –
The sounds that for these fifty years have been.

The whisper of the aspens is not drowned,
And over lightless pane and footless road,
Empty as sky, with every other sound
Not ceasing, calls their ghosts from their abode,

A silent smithy, a silent inn, nor fails
In the bare moonlight or the thick-furred gloom,
In tempest or the night of nightingales,
To turn the cross-roads to a ghostly room.

And it would be the same were no house near.
Over all sorts of weather, men, and times,
Aspens must shake their leaves and men may hear
But need not listen, more than to my rhymes.   20

Whatever wind blows, while they and I have leaves
We cannot other than an aspen be
That ceaselessly, unreasonably grieves,
Or so men think who like a different tree.

EDWARD THOMAS

The Great Lover

I have been so great a lover: filled my days
So proudly with the splendour of Love's praise,
The pain, the calm, and the astonishment,
Desire illimitable, and still content,
And all dear names men use, to cheat despair,
For the perplexed and viewless streams that bear
Our hearts at random down the dark of life.
Now, ere the unthinking silence on that strife
Steals down, I would cheat drowsy Death so far,
My night shall be remembered for a star   10
That outshone all the suns of all men's days.
Shall I not crown them with immortal praise
Whom I have loved, who have given me, dared with me
High secrets, and in darkness knelt to see
The inenarrable godhead of delight?   13

Love is a flame: — we have beaconed the world's night.
A city: — and we have built it, these and I.
An emperor: — we have taught the world to die.
So, for their sakes I loved, ere I go hence,
And the high cause of Love's magnificence,
And to keep loyalties young, I'll write those names
Golden for ever, eagles, crying flames,
And set them as a banner, that men may know,
To dare the generations, burn, and blow
Out on the wind of Time, shining and streaming . . .
These I have loved:

　　　　　　　　White plates and cups, clean-gleaming,
Ringed with blue lines; and feathery, faery dust;
Wet roofs, beneath the lamp-light; the strong crusts
Of friendly bread; and many-tasting food;
Rainbows; and the blue bitter smoke of wood;
And radiant raindrops couching in cool flowers;
And flowers themselves, that sway through sunny hours,
Dreaming of moths that drink them under the moon;
Then, the cool kindliness of sheets, that soon
Smooth away trouble; and the rough male kiss
Of blankets; grainy wood; live hair that is
Shining and free; blue-massing clouds; the keen
Unpassioned beauty of a great machine;
The benison of hot water; furs to touch;
The good smell of old clothes; and others such —
The comfortable smell of friendly fingers,
Hair's fragrance, and the musty reek that lingers
About dead leaves and last year's ferns . . .

　　　　　　　　　　　　　　　　Dear names,

And thousand other throng to me! Royal flames;
Sweet water's dimpling laugh from tap or spring;
Holes in the ground; and voices that do sing;
Voices in laughter, too; and body's pain,
Soon turned to peace; and the deep-panting train;
Firm sands; the little dulling edge of foam   *50*
That browns and dwindles as the wave goes home;
And washen stones, gay for an hour; the cold
Graveness of iron; moist black earthen mould,
Sleep; and high places; footprints in the dew;
And oaks; and brown horse-chestnuts, glossy-new;
And new-peeled sticks; and shining pools on grass; —
All these have been my loves. And these shall pass,
Whatever passes not, in the great hour,
Nor all my passion, all my prayers, have power
To hold them with me through the gate of Death.   *60*
They'll play deserter, turn with the traitor breath,
Break the high bond we made, and sell Love's trust
And sacramented covenant to the dust.
— Oh, never a doubt but, somewhere, I shall wake,
And give what's left of love again, and make
New friends, now strangers . . .

                 But the best I've known
Stays here, and changes, breaks, grows old, is blown
About the winds of the world, and fades from brains
Of living men, and dies.   *70*
               Nothing remains.

O dear my loves, O faithless, once again
This one last gift I give: that after men

Shall know, and later lovers, far-removed,
Praise you, 'All these were lovely'; say, 'He loved.'

RUPERT BROOKE

In Time of 'The Breaking of Nations'

Only a man harrowing clods
    In a slow silent walk
With an old horse that stumbles and nods
    Half asleep as they stalk.

Only thin smoke without flame
    From the heaps of couch-grass;
Yet this will go onward the same
    Though Dynasties pass.

Yonder a maid and her wight
    Come whispering by:
War's annals will cloud into night
    Ere their story die.

THOMAS HARDY

September 1913

What need you, being come to sense,
But fumble in a greasy till
And add the halfpence to the pence
And prayer to shivering prayer, until
You have dried the marrow from the bone;

For men were born to pray and save:
Romantic Ireland's dead and gone,
It's with O'Leary in the grave.

Yet they were of a different kind,
The names that stilled your childish play,   *10*
They have gone about the world like wind,
But little time had they to pray
For whom the hangman's rope was spun,
And what, God help us, could they save?
Romantic Ireland's dead and gone,
It's with O'Leary in the grave.

Was it for this the wild geese spread
The grey wing upon every tide;
For this that all that blood was shed,
For this Edward Fitzgerald died,   *20*
And Robert Emmet and Wolfe Tone,
All that delirium of the brave?
Romantic Ireland's dead and gone,
It's with O'Leary in the grave.

Yet could we turn the years again,
And call those exiles as they were
In all their loneliness and pain,
You'd cry, 'Some woman's yellow hair
Has maddened every mother's son':
They weighed so lightly what they gave.   *30*
But let them be, they're dead and gone,
They're with O'Leary in the grave.

The Voice

Woman much missed, how you call to me, call to me,
Saying that now you are not as you were
When you had changed from the one who was all to me,
But as at first, when our day was fair.

Can it be you that I hear? Let me view you, then,
Standing as when I drew near to the town
Where you would wait for me: yes, as I knew you then,
Even to the original air-blue gown!

Or is it only the breeze, in its listlessness
Travelling across the wet mead to me here,
You being ever dissolved to wan wistlessness,
Heard no more again far or near?

      Thus I; faltering forward,
      Leaves around me falling,
Wind oozing thin through the thorn from norward,
      And the woman calling.

THOMAS HARDY

After a Journey

Hereto I come to view a voiceless ghost;
    Whither, O whither will its whim now draw me?
Up the cliff, down, till I'm lonely, lost,
    And the unseen waters' ejaculations awe me.

Where you will next be there's no knowing,
    Facing round about me everywhere,
        With your nut-coloured hair,
And gray eyes, and rose-flush coming and going.

Yes: I have re-entered your olden haunts at last;
    Through the years, through the dead scenes I have
        tracked you;
What have you now found to say of our past –
    Scanned across the dark space wherein I have lacked you?
Summer gave us sweets, but autumn wrought division?
    Things were not lastly as firstly well
        With us twain, you tell?
But all's closed now, despite Time's derision.

I see what you are doing: you are leading me on
    To the spots we knew when we haunted here together,
The waterfall, above which the mist-bow shone
    At the then fair hour in the then fair weather,
And the cave just under, with a voice still so hollow
    That it seems to call out to me from forty years ago,
        When you were all aglow,
And not the thin ghost that I now fraily follow!

Ignorant of what there is flitting here to see,
    The waked birds preen and the seals flop lazily,
Soon you will have, Dear, to vanish from me,
    For the stars close their shutters and the dawn whitens
        hazily.
Trust me, I mind not, though Life lours,
    The bringing me here; nay, bring me here again!

I am just the same as when
Our days were a joy, and our paths through flowers.

THOMAS HARDY

Down by the Salley Gardens

Down by the salley gardens my love and I did meet;
She passed the salley gardens with little snow-white feet.
She bid me take love easy, as the leaves grow on the tree;
But I, being young and foolish, with her would not agree.

In a field by the river my love and I did stand,
And on my leaning shoulder she laid her snow-white hand.
She bid me take life easy, as the grass grows on the weirs;
But I was young and foolish, and now am full of tears.

WILLIAM BUTLER YEATS

At Castle Boterel

As I drive to the junction of lane and highway,
    And the drizzle bedrenches the waggonette,
I look behind at the fading byway,
    And see on its slope, now glistening wet,
        Distinctly yet

Myself and a girlish form benighted
    In dry March weather. We climb the road
Beside a chaise. We had just alighted
    To ease the sturdy pony's load
        When he sighed and slowed.

What we did as we climbed, and what we talked of
  Matters not much, nor to what it led, –
Something that life will not be balked of
  Without rude reason till hope is dead,
     And feeling fled.

It filled but a minute. But was there ever
  A time of such quality, since or before,
In that hill's story? To one mind never,
  Though it has been climbed, foot-swift, foot-sore,
     By thousands more.   20

Primaeval rocks form the road's steep border,
  And much have they faced there, first and last,
Of the transitory in Earth's long order;
  But what they record in colour and cast
     Is – that we two passed.

And to me, though Time's unflinching rigour,
  In mindless rote, has ruled from sight
The substance now, one phantom figure
  Remains on the slope, as when that night
     Saw us alight.   30

I look and see it there, shrinking, shrinking,
  I look back at it amid the rain
For the very last time; for my sand is sinking,
  And I shall traverse old love's domain
     Never again.

THOMAS HARDY

Tall Nettles

Tall nettles cover up, as they have done
These many springs, the rusty harrow, the plough
Long worn out, and the roller made of stone:
Only the elm butt tops the nettles now.

This corner of the farmyard I like most:
As well as any bloom upon a flower
I like the dust on the nettles, never lost
Except to prove the sweetness of a shower.

EDWARD THOMAS

The Poor Man's Pig

Already fallen plum-bloom stars the green,
   And apple-boughs as knarred as old toads' backs
Wear their small roses ere a rose is seen;
   The building thrush watches old Job who stacks
The fresh-peeled osiers on the sunny fence,
   The pent sow grunts to hear him stumping by,
And tries to push the bolt and scamper thence,
   But her ringed snout still keeps her to the sty.

Then out he lets her run; away she snorts
   In bundling gallop for the cottage door,
With hungry hubbub begging crusts and orts,
   Then like the whirlwind bumping round once more;

Nuzzling the dog, making the pullets run,
And sulky as a child when her play's done.

EDMUND BLUNDEN

Ringsend

[AFTER READING TOLSTOI]

I will live in Ringsend
With a red-headed whore,
And the fanlight gone in
Where it lights the hall-door;
And listen each night
For her querulous shout,
As at last she streels in
And the pubs empty out.
To soothe that wild breast
With my old-fangled songs,   *10*
Till she feels it redressed
From inordinate wrongs,
Imagined, outrageous,
Preposterous wrongs,
Till peace at last comes,
Shall be all I will do,
Where the little lamp blooms
Like a rose in the stew;
And up the back garden
The sound comes to me

Of the lapsing, unsoilable,
Whispering sea.

OLIVER ST JOHN GOGARTY

He Never Expected Much

A CONSIDERATION ON MY EIGHTY-SIXTH BIRTHDAY

Well, World, you have kept faith with me,
      Kept faith with me;
Upon the whole you have proved to be
      Much as you said you were.
Since as a child I used to lie
Upon the leaze and watch the sky,
Never, I own, expected I
      That life would all be fair.

'Twas then you said, and since have said,
      Times since have said,
In that mysterious voice you shed
      From clouds and hills around:
'Many have loved me desperately,
Many with smooth serenity,
While some have shown contempt of me
      Till they dropped underground.

'I do not promise overmuch,
      Child; overmuch;
Just neutral-tinted haps and such,'
      You said to minds like mine.

10

24

Wise warning for your credit's sake!
Which I for one failed not to take,
And hence could stem such strain and ache
        As each year might assign.

THOMAS HARDY

'Cities and Thrones and Powers'

Cities and Thrones and Powers
    Stand in Time's eye,
Almost as long as flowers,
    Which daily die:
But, as new buds put forth
    To glad new men,
Out of the spent and unconsidered Earth
    The Cities rise again.

This season's Daffodil
    She never hears   10
What change, what chance, what chill,
    Cut down last year's;
But with bold countenance,
    And knowledge small,
Esteems her seven days' continuance
    To be perpetual.

So Time that is o'erkind
    To all that be,
Ordains us e'en as blind,
    As bold as she:

That in our very death,
 And burial sure,
Shadow to shadow, well persuaded, saith,
 'See how our works endure!'

RUDYARD KIPLING

from *A Shropshire Lad*

XL

Into my heart an air that kills
 From yon far country blows:
What are those blue remembered hills,
 What spires, what farms are those?

That is the land of lost content,
 I see it shining plain,
The happy highways where I went
 And cannot come again.

A. E. HOUSMAN

The Way Through the Woods

They shut the road through the woods
Seventy years ago.
Weather and rain have undone it again,
And now you would never know
There was once a road through the woods
Before they planted the trees.

It is underneath the coppice and heath
And the thin anemones.
Only the keeper sees
That, where the ring-dove broods,
And the badgers roll at ease,   10
There was once a road through the woods.

Yet, if you enter the woods
Of a summer evening late,
When the night-air cools on the trout-ringed pools
Where the otter whistles his mate,
(They fear not men in the woods,
Because they see so few.)
You will hear the beat of a horse's feet,
And the swish of a skirt in the dew,   20
Steadily cantering through
The misty solitudes,
As though they perfectly knew
The old lost road through the woods . . .
But there is no road through the woods!

RUDYARD KIPLING

The Unknown Bird

Three lovely notes he whistled, too soft to be heard
If others sang; but others never sang
In the great beech-wood all that May and June.
No one saw him: I alone could hear him
Though many listened. Was it but four years
Ago? or five? He never came again.   27

Oftenest when I heard him I was alone,
Nor could I ever make another hear.
La-la-la! he called, seeming far-off –
As if a cock crowed past the edge of the world,
As if the bird or I were in a dream.
Yet that he travelled through the trees and sometimes
Neared me, was plain, though somehow distant still
He sounded. All the proof is – I told men
What I had heard.

              I never knew a voice,
Man, beast, or bird, better than this. I told
The naturalists; but neither had they heard
Anything like the notes that did so haunt me,
I had them clear by heart and have them still.
Four years, or five, have made no difference. Then
As now that La-la-la! was bodiless sweet:
Sad more than joyful it was, if I must say
That it was one or other, but if sad
'Twas sad only with joy too, too far off
For me to taste it. But I cannot tell
If truly never anything but fair
The days were when he sang, as now they seem.
This surely I know, that I who listened then,
Happy sometimes, sometimes suffering
A heavy body and a heavy heart,
Now straightway, if I think of it, become
Light as that bird wandering beyond my shore.

EDWARD THOMAS

from *A Shropshire Lad*

II

Loveliest of trees, the cherry now
Is hung with bloom along the bough,
And stands about the woodland ride
Wearing white for Eastertide.

Now, of my threescore years and ten,
Twenty will not come again,
And take from seventy springs a score,
It only leaves me fifty more.

And since to look at things in bloom
Fifty springs are little room,   *10*
About the woodlands I will go
To see the cherry hung with snow.

A. E. HOUSMAN

from *A Shropshire Lad*

XXXI

On Wenlock Edge the wood's in trouble;
   His forest fleece the Wrekin heaves;
The gale, it plies the saplings double,
   And thick on Severn snow the leaves.

'Twould blow like this through holt and hanger
   When Uricon the city stood:

'Tis the old wind in the old anger,
    But then it threshed another wood.

Then, 'twas before my time, the Roman
    At yonder heaving hill would stare:
The blood that warms an English yeoman,
    The thoughts that hurt him, they were there.

There, like the wind through woods in riot,
    Through him the gale of life blew high;
The tree of man was never quiet:
    Then 'twas the Roman, now 'tis I.

The gale, it plies the saplings double,
    It blows so hard, 'twill soon be gone:
To-day the Roman and his trouble
    Are ashes under Uricon.

A. E. HOUSMAN

from *A Shropshire Lad*

XXVII

'Is my team ploughing,
    That I was used to drive
And hear the harness jingle
    When I was man alive?'

Ay, the horses trample,
    The harness jingles now;
No change though you lie under
    The land you used to plough.

'Is football playing
    Along the river shore,
With lads to chase the leather,
    Now I stand up no more?'

Ay, the ball is flying,
    The lads play heart and soul;
The goal stands up, the keeper
    Stands up to keep the goal.

'Is my girl happy,
    That I thought hard to leave,
And has she tired of weeping
    As she lies down at eve?'

Ay, she lies down lightly,
    She lies not down to weep:
Your girl is well-contented.
    Be still, my lad, and sleep.

'Is my friend hearty,
    Now I am thin and pine,
And has he found to sleep in
    A better bed than mine?'

Yes, lad, I lie easy,
    I lie as lads would choose;
I cheer a dead man's sweetheart,
    Never ask me whose.

                    A. E. HOUSMAN

from *A Shropshire Lad*

LIV

With rue my heart is laden
  For golden friends I had,
For many a rose-lipt maiden
  And many a lightfoot lad.

By brooks too broad for leaping
  The lightfoot boys are laid;
The rose-lipt girls are sleeping
  In fields where roses fade.

A. E. HOUSMAN

from *A Shropshire Lad*

XXXII

From far, from eve and morning
  And yon twelve-winded sky,
The stuff of life to knit me
  Blew hither: here am I.

Now – for a breath I tarry
  Nor yet disperse apart –
Take my hand quick and tell me,
  What have you in your heart.

Speak now, and I will answer;
 How shall I help you, say;
Ere to the wind's twelve quarters
 I take my endless way.

The Magi

Now as at all times I can see in the mind's eye,
In their stiff, painted clothes, the pale unsatisfied ones
Appear and disappear in the blue depth of the sky
With all their ancient faces like rain-beaten stones,
And all their helms of silver hovering side by side,
And all their eyes still fixed, hoping to find once more,
Being by Calvary's turbulence unsatisfied,
The uncontrollable mystery on the bestial floor.

WILLIAM BUTLER YEATS

from *A Shropshire Lad*

IX

It is a fearful thing to be
 The Pope.
That cross will not be laid on me,
 I hope.
A righteous God would not permit
 It.

The Pope himself must often say,
After the labours of the day,
'It is a fearful thing to be
                              Me.'

A. E. HOUSMAN

Piano

Softly, in the dusk, a woman is singing to me;
Taking me back down the vista of years, till I see
A child sitting under the piano, in the boom of the tingling
     strings
And pressing the small, poised feet of a mother who smiles
     as she sings.

In spite of myself, the insidious mastery of song
Betrays me back, till the heart of me weeps to belong
To the old Sunday evenings at home, with winter outside
And hymns in the cosy parlour, the tinkling piano our
     guide.

So now it is vain for the singer to burst into clamour
With the great black piano appassionato. The glamour
Of childish days is upon me, my manhood is cast
Down in the flood of remembrance, I weep like a child for
     the past.

D. H. LAWRENCE

Sonnet Reversed

Hand trembling towards hand; the amazing lights
Of heart and eye. They stood on supreme heights.
Ah, the delirious weeks of honeymoon!
    Soon they returned, and, after strange adventures,
Settled at Balham by the end of June.
    Their money was in Can. Pacs. B. Debentures,
And in Antofagastas. Still he went
    Cityward daily; still she did abide
At home. And both were really quite content
    With work and social pleasures. Then they died.   *10*
They left three children (besides George, who drank):
    The eldest Jane, who married Mr Bell,
William, the head-clerk in the County Bank,
    And Henry, a stock-broker, doing well.

RUPERT BROOKE

The Rolling English Road

Before the Roman came to Rye or out to Severn strode,
The rolling English drunkard made the rolling English
    road.
A reeling road, a rolling road, that rambles round the shire,
And after him the parson ran, the sexton and the squire;
A merry road, a mazy road, and such as we did tread
The night we went to Birmingham by way of Beachy
    Head.

I knew no harm of Bonaparte and plenty of the Squire,
And for to fight the Frenchman I did not much desire;
But I did bash their baggonets because they came arrayed
To straighten out the crooked road an English drunkard
    made,
Where you and I went down the lane with ale-mugs in our
    hands,
The night we went to Glastonbury by way of Goodwin
    Sands.

His sins they were forgiven him; or why do flowers run
Behind him; and the hedges all strengthening in the sun?
The wild thing went from left to right and knew not which
    was which,
But the wild rose was above him when they found him in the
    ditch.
God pardon us, nor harden us; we did not see so clear
The night we went to Bannockburn by way of Brighton
    Pier.

My friends, we will not go again or ape an ancient rage,
Or stretch the folly of our youth to be the shame of age,
But walk with clearer eyes and ears this path that
    wandereth,
And see undrugged in evening light the decent inn of
    death;
For there is good news yet to hear and fine things to be seen,
Before we go to Paradise by way of Kensal Green.

G. K. CHESTERTON

The Listeners

'Is there anybody there?' said the Traveller,
  Knocking on the moonlit door;
And his horse in the silence champed the grasses
  Of the forest's ferny floor:
And a bird flew up out of the turret,
  Above the Traveller's head:
And he smote upon the door again a second time;
  'Is there anybody there?' he said.
But no one descended to the Traveller;
  No head from the leaf-fringed sill
Leaned over and looked into his grey eyes,
  Where he stood perplexed and still.
But only a host of phantom listeners
  That dwelt in the lone house then
Stood listening in the quiet of the moonlight
  To that voice from the world of men:
Stood thronging the faint moonbeams on the dark stair,
  That goes down to the empty hall,
Hearkening in an air stirred and shaken
  By the lonely Traveller's call.
And he felt in his heart their strangeness,
  Their stillness answering his cry,
While his horse moved, cropping the dark turf,
  'Neath the starred and leafy sky;
For he suddenly smote on the door, even
  Louder, and lifted his head: –

'Tell them I came, and no one answered,
    That I kept my word,' he said.
Never the least stir made the listeners,
    Though every word he spake
Fell echoing through the shadowiness of the still house
    From the one man left awake:
Ay, they heard his foot upon the stirrup,
    And the sound of iron on stone,
And how the silence surged softly backward,
    When the plunging hoofs were gone.

WALTER DE LA MARE

Lights Out

I have come to the borders of sleep,
The unfathomable deep
Forest where all must lose
Their way, however straight,
Or winding, soon or late;
They cannot choose.

Many a road and track
That, since the dawn's first crack,
Up to the forest brink,
Deceived the travellers,
Suddenly now blurs,
And in they sink.

Here love ends,
Despair, ambition ends;

All pleasure and all trouble,
Although most sweet or bitter,
Here ends in sleep that is sweeter
Than tasks most noble.

There is not any book
Or face of dearest look
That I would not turn from now   20
To go into the unknown
I must enter, and leave, alone,
I know not how.

The tall forest towers;
Its cloudy foliage lowers
Ahead, shelf above shelf;
Its silence I hear and obey
That I may lose my way
And myself.   30

EDWARD THOMAS

The Little Dog's Day

All in the town were still asleep,
When the sun came up with a shout and a leap.
In the lonely streets unseen by man,
A little dog danced. And the day began.

All his life he'd been good, as far as he could,
And the poor little beast had done all that he should.   39

But this morning he swore, by Odin and Thor
And the Canine Valhalla – he'd stand it no more!

So his prayer he got granted – to do just what he wanted,
Prevented by none, for the space of one day.
'*Jam incipiebo, sedere facebo,*'
In dog-Latin he quoth, '*Euge! sophos! hurray!*'

He fought with the he-dogs, and winked at the she-dogs,
A thing that had never been *heard* of before.
'For the stigma of gluttony, I care not a button!' he
Cried, and ate all he could swallow – and more.

He took sinewy lumps from the shins of old frumps,
And mangled the errand-boys – when he could get 'em.
He shammed furious *rabies*, and bit all the babies,
And followed the cats up the trees, and then ate 'em!

They thought 'twas the devil was holding a revel,
And sent for the parson to drive him away;
For the town never knew such a hullabaloo
As that little dog raised – till the end of that day.

> *When the blood-red sun had gone burning down,*
> *And the lights were lit in the little town,*
> *Outside, in the gloom of the twilight grey,*
> *The little dog died when he'd had his day.*

RUPERT BROOKE

The Old Vicarage, Grantchester

Just now the lilac is in bloom,
All before my little room;
And in my flower-beds, I think,
Smile the carnation and the pink;
And down the borders, well I know,
The poppy and the pansy blow . . .
Oh! there the chestnuts, summer through,
Beside the river make for you
A tunnel of green gloom, and sleep
Deeply above; and green and deep   *10*
The stream mysterious glides beneath,
Green as a dream and deep as death.
– Oh, damn! I know it! and I know
How the May fields all golden show,
And when the day is young and sweet,
Gild gloriously the bare feet
That run to bathe . . .

           Du lieber Gott!

Here am I, sweating, sick, and hot,
And there the shadowed waters fresh   *20*
Lean up to embrace the naked flesh.
Temperamentvoll German Jews
Drink beer around; – and *there* the dews
Are soft beneath a morn of gold.
Here tulips bloom as they are told;
Unkempt about those hedges blows

An English unofficial rose;
And there the unregulated sun
Slopes down to rest when day is done,
And wakes a vague unpunctual star,
A slippered Hesper; and there are
Meads towards Haslingfield and Coton
Where *das Betreten*'s not *verboten*.

εἴθε γενοίμην . . . would I were
In Grantchester, in Grantchester! –
Some, it may be, can get in touch
With Nature there, or Earth, or such.
And clever modern men have seen
A Faun a-peeping through the green,
And felt the Classics were not dead,
To glimpse a Naiad's reedy head,
Or hear the Goat-foot piping low: . . .
But these are things I do not know.
I only know that you may lie
Day-long and watch the Cambridge sky,
And, flower-lulled in sleepy grass,
Hear the cool lapse of hours pass,
Until the centuries blend and blur
In Grantchester, in Grantchester . . .
Still in the dawnlit waters cool
His ghostly Lordship swims his pool,
And tries the strokes, essays the tricks,
Long learnt on Hellespont, or Styx.
Dan Chaucer hears his river still
Chatter beneath a phantom mill.

Tennyson notes, with studious eye,
How Cambridge waters hurry by . . .
And in that garden, black and white,
Creep whispers through the grass all night;
And spectral dance, before the dawn,   60
A hundred Vicars down the lawn;
Curates, long dust, will come and go
On lissom, clerical, printless toe;
And oft between the boughs is seen
The sly shade of a Rural Dean . . .
Till, at a shiver in the skies,
Vanishing with Satanic cries,
The prim ecclesiastic rout
Leaves but a startled sleeper-out,
Grey heavens, the first bird's drowsy calls,   70
The falling house that never falls.

God! I will pack, and take a train,
And get me to England once again!
For England's the one land, I know,
Where men with Splendid Hearts may go;
And Cambridgeshire, of all England,
The shire for Men who Understand;
And of *that* district I prefer
The lovely hamlet Grantchester.
For Cambridge people rarely smile,   80
Being urban, squat, and packed with guile;
And Royston men in the far South
Are black and fierce and strange of mouth;
At Over they fling oaths at one,

And worse than oaths at Trumpington,
And Ditton girls are mean and dirty,
And there's none in Harston under thirty,
And folks in Shelford and those parts
Have twisted lips and twisted hearts,
And Barton men make Cockney rhymes,
And Coton's full of nameless crimes,
And things are done you'd not believe
At Madingley, on Christmas Eve.
Strong men have run for miles and miles,
When one from Cherry Hinton smiles;
Strong men have blanched, and shot their wives,
Rather than send them to St Ives;
Strong men have cried like babes, bydam,
To hear what happened at Babraham.
But Grantchester! ah, Grantchester!
There's peace and holy quiet there,
Great clouds along pacific skies,
And men and women with straight eyes,
Lithe children lovelier than a dream,
A bosky wood, a slumbrous stream,
And little kindly winds that creep
Round twilight corners, half asleep.
In Grantchester their skins are white;
They bathe by day, they bathe by night;
The women there do all they ought;
The men observe the Rules of Thought.
They love the Good; they worship Truth;
They laugh uproariously in youth;
(And when they get to feeling old,

They up and shoot themselves, I'm told) . . .

Ah God! to see the branches stir
Across the moon at Grantchester!
To smell the thrilling-sweet and rotten
Unforgettable, unforgotten
River-smell, and hear the breeze
Sobbing in the little trees.
Say, do the elm-clumps greatly stand
Still guardians of that holy land?
The chestnuts shade, in reverend dream,
The yet unacademic stream?
Is dawn a secret shy and cold
Anadyomene, silver-gold?
And sunset still a golden sea
From Haslingfield to Madingley?
And after, ere the night is born,
Do hares come out about the corn?
Oh, is the water sweet and cool,
Gentle and brown, above the pool?
And laughs the immortal river still
Under the mill, under the mill?
Say, is there Beauty yet to find?
And Certainty? and Quiet kind?
Deep meadows yet, for to forget
The lies, and truths, and pain? . . . Oh! yet
Stands the Church clock at ten to three?
And is there honey still for tea?

RUPERT BROOKE

Sea Fever

I must go down to the seas again, to the lonely sea and the sky,
And all I ask is a tall ship and a star to steer her by;
And the wheel's kick and the wind's song and the white
    sail's shaking,
And a grey mist on the sea's face, and a grey dawn breaking.

I must go down to the seas again, for the call of the
    running tide
Is a wild call and a clear call that may not be denied;
And all I ask is a windy day with the white clouds flying,
and the flung spray and the blown spume, and the sea-
    gulls crying.

I must go down to the seas again, to the vagrant
    gypsy life,
To the gull's way and the whale's way where the wind's
    like a whetted knife;
And all I ask is a merry yarn from a laughing fellow-rover,
And quiet sleep and a sweet dream when the long trick's over.

JOHN MASEFIELD

Cargoes

Quinquireme of Nineveh from distant Ophir
Rowing home to haven in sunny Palestine,
With a cargo of ivory,
And apes and peacocks,
Sandalwood, cedarwood, and sweet white wine.

Stately Spanish galleon coming from the Isthmus,
Dipping through the Tropics by the palm-green shores,
With a cargo of diamonds,
Emeralds, amethysts,
Topazes, and cinnamon, and gold moidores.   *10*

Dirty British coaster with a salt-caked smoke stack
Butting through the channel in the mad March days,
With a cargo of Tyne coal,
Road-rail, pig-lead,
Firewood, iron-ware, and cheap tin trays.

JOHN MASEFIELD

Mandalay

By the old Moulmein Pagoda, lookin' eastward to the sea,
There's a Burma girl a-settin', an' I know she thinks o' me;
For the wind is in the palm-trees, an' the temple-bells they
    say:
'Come you back, you British soldier; come you back to
    Mandalay!'
  Come you back to Mandalay,
  Where the old Flotilla lay:
  Can't you 'ear their paddles chunkin' from Rangoon to
    Mandalay?
  On the road to Mandalay,
  Where the flyin'-fishes play,
  An' the dawn comes up like thunder outer China 'crost   *10*
    the Bay!

'Er petticoat was yaller an' 'er little cap was green,
An' 'er name was Supi-yaw-lat – jes' the same as Theebaw's
    Queen,
An' I seed her first a-smokin' of a whackin' white cheroot,
An' a-wastin' Christian kisses on an 'eathen idol's foot:
  Bloomin' idol made o' mud –
  Wot they called the Great Gawd Budd –
  Plucky lot she cared for idols when I kissed 'er where
      she stud!
  On the road to Mandalay . . .

When the mist was on the rice-fields an' the sun was
    droppin' slow,
She'd git 'er little banjo an' she'd sing '*Kulla-lo-lo!*'
With 'er arm upon my shoulder an' 'er cheek agin my
    cheek
We useter watch the steamers an' the *hathis* pilin' teak.
  Elephints a-pilin' teak
  In the sludgy, squdgy creek,
  Where the silence 'ung that 'eavy you was 'arf afraid to
      speak!
  On the road to Mandalay . . .

But that's all shove be'ind me – long ago an' fur away,
An' there ain't no 'buses runnin' from the Bank to Mandalay;
An' I'm learnin' 'ere in London what the ten-year soldier tells:
'If you've 'eard the East a-callin', you won't never 'eed
    naught else.'
  No! you won't 'eed nothin' else
  But them spicy garlic smells,

    An' the sunshine an' the palm-trees an' the tinkly temple
       bells;
    On the road to Mandalay . . .

I am sick o' wastin' leather on these gritty pavin'-stones,
An' the blasted English drizzle wakes the fever in my bones;
Tho' I walks with fifty 'ousemaids outer Chelsea to the
      Strand,
An' they talks a lot o' lovin', but wot do they understand?
    Beefy face an' grubby 'and –
    Law! wot do they understand?   *40*
    I've a neater, sweeter maiden in a cleaner, greener land!
    On the road to Mandalay . . .

Ship me somewheres east of Suez, where the best is like
      the worst,
Where there aren't no Ten Commandments an' a man can
      raise a thirst;
For the temple-bells are callin', an' it's there that I would be –
By the old Moulmein Pagoda, looking lazy at the sea;
    On the road to Mandalay,
    Where the old Flotilla lay,
    With our sick beneath the awnings when we went to
      Mandalay!
    Oh, the road to Mandalay,   *50*
    Where the flyin'-fishes play,
    An' the dawn comes up like thunder outer China 'crost
      the Bay!

RUDYARD KIPLING

The Mary Gloster

I've paid for your sickest fancies; I've humoured your
    crackedest whim –
Dick, it's your daddy, dying; you've got to listen to him!
Good for a fortnight, am I? The doctor told you? He lied.
I shall go under by morning, and – Put that nurse outside.
Never seen death yet, Dickie? Well, now is your time to
    learn,
And you'll wish you held my record before it comes to
    your turn.
Not counting the Line and the Foundry, the Yards and the
    village, too,
I've made myself and a million; but I'm damned if I made
    you.
Master at two-and-twenty, and married at twenty-three –
Ten thousand men on the pay-roll, and forty freighters at
    sea!
Fifty years between 'em, and every year of it fight,
And now I'm Sir Anthony Gloster, dying, a baronite:
For I lunched with his Royal 'Ighness – what was it the
    papers had?
'Not least of our merchant-princes.' Dickie, that's me, your
    dad!
I didn't begin with askings. *I* took my job and I stuck;
I took the chances they wouldn't, an' now they're calling it
    luck.
Lord, what boats I've handled – rotten and leaky and old –
Ran 'em, or – opened the bilge-cock, precisely as I was told.

Grub that 'ud bind you crazy, and crews that 'ud turn you
 grey,
And a big fat lump of insurance to cover the risk on the way. 20
The others they dursn't do it; they said they valued their life
(They've served me since as skippers). *I* went, and I took
 my wife.
Over the world I drove 'em, married at twenty-three,
And your mother saving the money and making a man of
 me.
I was content to be master, but she said there was better
 behind;
She took the chances I wouldn't, and I followed your
 mother blind.
She egged me to borrow the money, an' she helped me to
 clear the loan,
When we bought half-shares in a cheap 'un and hoisted a
 flag of our own.
Patching and coaling on credit, and living the Lord knew
 how,
We started the Red Ox freighters – we've eight-and-thirty 30
 now.
And those were the days of clippers, and the freights were
 clipper-freights,
And we knew we were making our fortune, but she died in
 Macassar Straits –
By the Little Paternosters, as you come to the Union Bank –
And we dropped her in fourteen fathom: I pricked it off
 where she sank.
Owners we were, full owners, and the boat was christened
 for her,

And she died in the *Mary Gloster*. My heart, how young
  we were!
So I went on a spree round Java and wellnigh ran her
  ashore,
But your mother came and warned me and I wouldn't
  liquor no more:
Strict I stuck to my business, afraid to stop or I'd think,
Saving the money (she warned me), and letting the other
  men drink.
And I met M'Cullough in London (I'd saved five 'undred
  then),
And 'tween us we started the Foundry – three forges and
  twenty men.
Cheap repairs for the cheap 'uns. It paid, and the business
  grew;
For I bought me a steam-lathe patent, and that was a gold
  mine too.
'Cheaper to build 'em than buy 'em,' *I* said, but
  M'Cullough he shied,
And we wasted a year in talking before we moved to the
  Clyde.
And the Lines were all beginning, and we all of us started
  fair,
Building our engines like houses and staying the boilers
  square.
But M'Cullough 'e wanted cabins with marble and maple
  and all,
And Brussels an' Utrecht velvet, and baths and a Social
  Hall,
And pipes for closets all over, and cutting the frames too light,

But M'Cullough he died in the Sixties, and – Well, I'm
    dying to-night . . .
I knew – *I* knew what was coming, when we bid on the
    Byfleet's keel –
They piddled and piffled with iron. I'd given my orders
    for steel!
Steel and the first expansions. It paid, I tell you, it paid,
When we came with our nine-knot freighters and collared
    the long-run trade!
And they asked me how I did it, and I gave 'em the
    Scripture text,
'You keep your light so shining a little in front o' the next!'
They copied all they could follow, but they couldn't copy
    my mind,
And I left 'em sweating and stealing a year and a half
    behind.   60
Then came the armour-contracts, but that was
    M'Cullough's side;
He was always best in the Foundry, but better, perhaps, he
    died.
I went through his private papers; the notes was plainer
    than print;
And I'm no fool to finish if a man'll give me a hint.
(I remember his widow was angry.) So I saw what his
    drawings meant,
And I started the six-inch rollers, and it paid me sixty per
    cent.
Sixty per cent *with* failures, and more than twice we could
    do,
And a quarter-million to credit, and I saved it all for you!   53

I thought – it doesn't matter – you seemed to favour your
    ma,
70 But you're nearer forty than thirty, and I know the kind
    you are.
Harrer an' Trinity College! I ought to ha' sent you to sea –
But I stood you an education, an' what have you done for
    me?
The things I knew was proper you wouldn't thank me to
    give,
And the things I knew was rotten you said was the way to
    live.
For you muddled with books and pictures, an' china an'
    etchin's an' fans,
And your rooms at college was beastly – more like a
    whore's than a man's;
Till you married that thin-flanked woman, as white and as
    stale as a bone,
An' she gave you your social nonsense; but where's that kid
    o' your own?
I've seen your carriages blocking the half o' the Cromwell
    Road,
80 But never the doctor's brougham to help the missus
    unload.
(So there isn't even a grandchild, an' the Gloster family's
    done.)
Not like your mother, she isn't. *She* carried her freight
    each run.
But they died, the pore little beggars! At sea she had 'em –
    they died.
54 Only you, an' you stood it. You haven't stood much beside.

Weak, a liar, and idle, and mean as a collier's whelp
Nosing for scraps in the galley. No help – my son was no help!
So he gets three 'undred thousand, in trust and the interest
   paid.
I wouldn't give it you, Dickie – you see, I made it in trade.
You're saved from soiling your fingers, and if you have no
   child,
It all comes back to the business. 'Gad, won't your wife be   *90*
   wild!
Calls and calls in her carriage, her 'andkerchief up to 'er
   eye:
'Daddy! dear daddy's dyin'!' and doing her best to cry.
Grateful? Oh, yes, I'm grateful, but keep her away from
   here.
Your mother 'ud never ha' stood 'er, and, anyhow, women
   are queer . . .
There's women will say I've married a second time. Not
   quite!
But give pore Aggie a hundred, and tell her your lawyers'll
   fight.
She was the best o' the boiling – you'll meet her before it
   ends.
I'm in for a row with the mother – I'll leave you settle my
   friends.
For a man he must go with a woman, which women don't
   understand –
Or the sort that say they can see it they aren't the marrying   *100*
   brand.
But I wanted to speak o' your mother that's Lady Gloster
   still;

I'm going to up and see her, without its hurting the will.
Here! Take your hand off the bell-pull. Five thousand's
    waiting for you,
If you'll only listen a minute, and do as I bid you do.
They'll try to prove me crazy, and, if you bungle, they can;
And I've only you to trust to! (O God, why ain't it a man?)
There's some waste money on marbles, the same as
    M'Cullough tried –
Marbles and mausoleums – but I call that sinful pride.
There's some ship bodies for burial – we've carried 'em,
    soldered and packed;
Down in their wills they wrote it, and nobody called *them*
    cracked.
But me – I've too much money, and people might . . . All
    my fault:
It come o' hoping for grandsons and buying that Wokin'
    vault . . .
I'm sick o' the 'ole dam' business. I'm going back where I
    came.
Dick, you're the son o' my body, and you'll take charge o'
    the same!
I want to lie by your mother, ten thousand mile away,
And they'll want to send me to Woking; and that's where
    you'll earn your pay.
I've thought it out on the quiet, the same as it ought to be
    done –
Quiet, and decent, and proper – an' here's your orders, my
    son.
You know the Line? You don't, though. You write to the
    Board, and tell

Your father's death has upset you an' you're goin' to cruise   *120*
    for a spell,
An' you'd like the *Mary Gloster* – I've held her ready for
    this –
They'll put her in working order and you'll take her out as
    she is.
Yes, it was money idle when I patched her and laid her
    aside
(Thank God, I can pay for my fancies!) – the boat where
    your mother died,
By the Little Paternosters, as you come to the Union Bank,
We dropped her – I think I told you – and I pricked it off
    where she sank.
['Tiny she looked on the grating – that oily, treacly sea –]
'Hundred and Eighteen East, remember, and South just
    Three.
Easy bearings to carry – Three South – Three to the dot;
But I gave McAndrew a copy in case of dying – or not.   *130*
And so you'll write to McAndrew, he's Chief of the Maori
    Line;
They'll give him leave, if you ask 'em, and say it's business
    o' mine.
I built three boats for the Maoris, an' very well pleased
    they were,
An' I've known Mac since the Fifties, and Mac knew me –
    and her.
After the first stroke warned me I sent him the money to
    keep
Against the time you'd claim it, committin' your dad to the
    deep;

For you are the son o' my body, and Mac was my oldest
    friend,
I've never asked 'im to dinner, but he'll see it out to the
    end.
Stiff-necked Glasgow beggar! I've heard he's prayed for
    my soul,
But he couldn't lie if you paid him, and he'd starve before
    he stole.
He'll take the *Mary* in ballast – you'll find her a lively ship;
And you'll take Sir Anthony Gloster, that goes on 'is
    wedding-trip,
Lashed in our old deck-cabin with all three port-holes
    wide,
The kick o' the screw beneath him and the round blue seas
    outside!
Sir Anthony Gloster's carriage – our 'ouse-flag flyin' free –
Ten thousand men on the pay-roll and forty freighters at
    sea!
He made himself and a million, but this world is a fleetin'
    show,
And he'll go to the wife of 'is bosom the same as he ought
    to go –
By the heel of the Paternosters – there isn't a chance to
    mistake –
And Mac'll pay you the money as soon as the bubbles
    break!
Five thousand for six weeks' cruising, the staunchest
    freighter afloat,
And Mac he'll give you your bonus the minute I'm out o'
    the boat!

He'll take you round to Macassar, and you'll come back
   alone;
He knows what I want o' the *Mary* . . . I'll do what I
   please with my own.
Your mother 'ud call it wasteful, but I've seven-and-thirty
   more;
I'll come in my private carriage and bid it wait at the
   door . . .
For my son 'e was never a credit: 'e muddled with books
   and art,
And 'e lived on Sir Anthony's money and 'e broke Sir
   Anthony's heart.
There isn't even a grandchild, and the Gloster family's
   done –
The only one you left me – O mother, the only one!   160
Harrer and Trinity College – me slavin' early an' late –
An' he thinks I'm dying crazy, and you're in Macassar
   Strait!
Flesh o' my flesh, my dearie, for ever an' ever amen,
That first stroke come for a warning. I ought to ha' gone to
   you then.
But – cheap repairs for a cheap 'un – the doctors said I'd
   do.
Mary, why didn't *you* warn me? I've allus heeded to you,
Excep' – I know – about women; but you are a spirit now;
An', wife, they was only women, and I was a man. That's
   how.
An' a man 'e must go with a woman, as you *could* not
   understand;
But I never talked 'em secrets. I paid 'em out o' hand.

Thank Gawd, I can pay for my fancies! Now what's five
    thousand to me,
For a berth off the Paternosters in the haven where I
    would be?
I believe in the Resurrection, if I read my Bible plain,
But I wouldn't trust 'em at Wokin'; we're safer at sea
    again.
For the heart it shall go with the treasure – go down to the
    sea in ships.
I'm sick of the hired women. I'll kiss my girl on her lips!
I'll be content with my fountain. I'll drink from my own
    well,
And the wife of my youth shall charm me – an' the rest
    can go to Hell!
(Dickie, *he* will, that's certain.) I'll lie in our standin'-bed,
An' Mac'll take her in ballast – an' she trims best by the
    head . . .
Down by the head an' sinkin', her fires are drawn and cold,
And the water's splashin' hollow on the skin of the empty
    hold –
Churning an' choking and chuckling, quiet and scummy
    and dark –
Full to her lower hatches and risin' steady. Hark!
That was the after-bulkhead . . . She's flooded from stem
    to stern . . .
Never seen death yet, Dickie? . . . Well, now is your time
    to learn!

RUDYARD KIPLING

Danny Deever

'What are the bugles blowin' for?' said Files-on-Parade.
'To turn you out, to turn you out,' the Colour-Sergeant
said.
'What makes you look so white, so white?' said Files-on-
Parade.
'I'm dreadin' what I've got to watch,' the Colour-Sergeant
said.
   For they're hangin' Danny Deever, you can hear the
   Dead March play,
   The Regiment's in 'ollow square – they're hangin' him
   to-day;
   They've taken of his buttons off an' cut his stripes away,
   An' they're hangin' Danny Deever in the mornin'.

'What makes the rear-rank breathe so 'ard?' said Files-on-
Parade.
'It's bitter cold, it's bitter cold,' the Colour-Sergeant said.   10
'What makes that front-rank man fall down?' said Files-on-
Parade.
'A touch o' sun, a touch o' sun,' the Colour-Sergeant said.
   They are hangin' Danny Deever, they are marchin' of
   'im round,
   They 'ave 'alted Danny Deever by 'is coffin on the
   ground;
   An' 'e'll swing in 'arf a minute for a sneakin' shootin'
   hound –
   O they're hangin' Danny Deever in the mornin'!

''Is cot was right-'and cot to mine,' said Files-on-Parade.
''E's sleepin' out an' far to-night,' the Colour-Sergeant
said.
'I've drunk 'is beer a score o' times,' said Files-on-Parade.
''E's drinkin' bitter beer alone,' the Colour-Sergeant said.
    They are hangin' Danny Deever, you must mark 'im to
      'is place,
    For 'e shot a comrade sleepin' – you must look 'im in
      the face;
    Nine 'undred of 'is county an' the Regiment's disgrace,
    While they're hangin' Danny Deever in the mornin'.

'What's that so black agin the sun?' said Files-on-Parade.
'It's Danny fightin' 'ard for life,' the Colour-Sergeant said.
'What's that that whimpers over 'ead?' said Files-on-Parade.
'It's Danny's soul that's passin' now,' the Colour-Sergeant
said.
    For they're done with Danny Deever, you can 'ear the
      quickstep play,
    The Regiment's in column, an' they're marchin' us away;
    Ho! the young recruits are shakin', an' they'll want their
      beer to-day,
    After hangin' Danny Deever in the mornin'!

RUDYARD KIPLING

In Freiburg Station

In Freiburg station, waiting for a train,
I saw a Bishop in puce gloves go by.

Now God may thunder furious from the sky,
Shattering all my glory into pain,
And joy turn stinking rotten, hope be vain,
Night fall on little laughters, little loves,
And better Bishops don more glorious gloves,
While I go down in darkness; what care I?

There is one memory God can never break,
There is one splendour more than all the pain,   *10*
There is one secret that shall never die,
Star-crowned I stand and sing, for that hour's sake.
In Freiburg station, waiting for a train,
I saw a Bishop with puce gloves go by.

RUPERT BROOKE

from *A Shropshire Lad*

XVI

It nods and curtseys and recovers
    When the wind blows above,
The nettle on the graves of lovers
    That hanged themselves for love.

The nettle nods, the wind blows over,
    The man, he does not move,
The lover of the grave, the lover
    That hanged himself for love.

A. E. HOUSMAN

Adlestrop

Yes. I remember Adlestrop –
The name, because one afternoon
Of heat the express-train drew up there
Unwontedly. It was late June.

The steam hissed. Someone cleared his throat.
No one left and no one came
On the bare platform. What I saw
Was Adlestrop – only the name

And willows, willow-herb, and grass,
And meadowsweet, and haycocks dry,
No whit less still and lonely fair
Than the high cloudlets in the sky.

And for that minute a blackbird sang
Close by, and round him, mistier,
Farther and farther, all the birds
Of Oxfordshire and Gloucestershire.

EDWARD THOMAS

Song of a Man Who Has Come Through

Not I, not I, but the wind that blows through me!
A fine wind is blowing the new direction of Time.
If only I let it bear me, carry me, if only it carry me!
If only I am sensitive, subtle, oh, delicate, a winged gift!
If only, most lovely of all, I yield myself and am borrowed

By the fine, fine wind that takes its course through the
    chaos of the world
Like a fine, an exquisite chisel, a wedge-blade inserted;
If only I am keen and hard like the sheer tip of a wedge
Driven by invisible blows,
The rock will split, we shall come at the wonder, we shall
    find the Hesperides.

Oh, for the wonder that bubbles into my soul,
I would be a good fountain, a good well-head,
Would blur no whisper, spoil no expression.

What is the knocking?
What is the knocking at the door in the night?
It is somebody wants to do us harm.

No, no, it is the three strange angels.
Admit them, admit them.

                      D. H. LAWRENCE

Jealousy

When I see you, who were so wise and cool,
Gazing with silly sickness on that fool
You've given your love to, your adoring hands
Touch his so intimately that each understands,
I know, most hidden things; and when I know
Your holiest dreams yield to the stupid bow
Of his red lips, and that the empty grace
Of those strong legs and arms, that rosy face,
Has beaten your heart to such a flame of love,

65

That you have given him every touch and move,
Wrinkle and secret of you, all your life,
– Oh! then I know I'm waiting, lover-wife,
For the great time when love is at a close,
And all its fruit's to watch the thickening nose
And sweaty neck and dulling face and eye,
That are yours, and you, most surely, till you die!
Day after day you'll sit with him and note
The greasier tie, the dingy wrinkling coat;
As prettiness turns to pomp, and strength to fat,
And love, love, love to habit!

                    And after that,
When all that's fine in man is at an end,
And you, that loved young life and clean, must tend
A foul sick fumbling dribbling body and old,
When his rare lips hang flabby and can't hold
Slobber, and you're enduring that worst thing,
Senility's queasy furtive love-making,
And searching those dear eyes for human meaning,
Propping the bald and helpless head, and cleaning
A scrap that life's flung by, and love's forgotten, –
Then you'll be tired; and passion dead and rotten;
And he'll be dirty, dirty!

                    O lithe and free
And lightfoot, that the poor heart cries to see,
That's how I'll see your man and you! –

                                 But you
– Oh, when *that* time comes, you'll be dirty too!

RUPERT BROOKE

The Owl

Downhill I came, hungry, and yet not starved;
Cold, yet had heat within me that was proof
Against the North wind; tired, yet so that rest
Had seemed the sweetest thing under a roof.

Then at the inn I had food, fire, and rest,
Knowing how hungry, cold, and tired was I.
All of the night was quite barred out except
An owl's cry, a most melancholy cry

Shaken out long and clear upon the hill,
No merry note, nor cause of merriment,   *10*
But one telling me plain what I escaped
And others could not, that night, as in I went.

And salted was my food, and my repose,
Salted and sobered, too, by the bird's voice
Speaking for all who lay under the stars,
Soldiers and poor, unable to rejoice.

EDWARD THOMAS

Roads

I love roads:
The goddesses that dwell
Far along them invisible
Are my favourite gods.

Roads go on
While we forget, and are
Forgotten like a star
That shoots and is gone.

On this earth 'tis sure
We men have not made
Anything that doth fade
So soon, so long endure:

The hill road wet with rain
In the sun would not gleam
Like a winding stream
If we trod it not again.

They are lonely
While we sleep, lonelier
For lack of the traveller
Who is now a dream only.

From dawn's twilight
And all the clouds like sheep
On the mountains of sleep
They wind into the night.

The next turn may reveal
Heaven: upon the crest
The close pine clump, at rest
And black, may Hell conceal.

Often footsore, never
Yet of the road I weary,

Though long and steep and dreary,
As it winds on for ever.

Helen of the roads,
The mountain ways of Wales
And the Mabinogion tales
Is one of the true gods,

Abiding in the trees,
The threes and fours so wise,
The larger companies,
That by the roadside be,   40

And beneath the rafter
Else uninhabited
Excepting by the dead;
And it is her laughter

At morn and night I hear
When the thrush cock sings
Bright irrelevant things,
And when the chanticleer

Calls back to their own night
Troops that make loneliness   50
With their light footsteps' press,
As Helen's own are light.

Now all roads lead to France
And heavy is the tread
Of the living; but the dead
Returning lightly dance:

Whatever the road bring
To me or take from me,
They keep me company
With their pattering,

Crowding the solitude
Of the loops over the downs,
Hushing the roar of towns
And their brief multitude.

EDWARD THOMAS

Report on Experience

I have been young, and now am not too old;
And I have seen the righteous forsaken,
His health, his honour and his quality taken.
    This is not what we were formerly told.

I have seen a green country, useful to the race,
Knocked silly with guns and mines, its villages vanished,
Even the last rat and last kestrel banished –
    God bless us all, this was peculiar grace.

I knew Seraphina; Nature gave her hue,
Glance, sympathy, note, like one from Eden.
I saw her smile warp, heard her lyric deaden;
    She turned to harlotry; – this I took to be new.

Say what you will, our God sees how they run.
These disillusions are his curious proving
That he loves humanity and will go on loving;
  Over there are faith, life, virtue in the sun.

EDMUND BLUNDEN

from *1914*

V THE SOLDIER

If I should die, think only this of me:
  That there's some corner of a foreign field
That is for ever England. There shall be
  In that rich earth a richer dust concealed;
A dust whom England bore, shaped, made aware,
  Gave, once, her flowers to love, her ways to roam,
A body of England's, breathing English air,
  Washed by the rivers, blest by suns of home.

And think, this heart, all evil shed away,
  A pulse in the eternal mind, no less   *10*
    Gives somewhere back the thoughts by England
      given;
Her sights and sounds; dreams happy as her day;
  And laughter, learnt of friends; and gentleness,
    In hearts at peace, under an English heaven.

RUPERT BROOKE

Everyone Sang

Everyone suddenly burst out singing;
And I was filled with such delight
As prisoned birds must find in freedom,
Winging wildly across the white
Orchards and dark-green fields; on – on – and out of sight.

Everyone's voice was suddenly lifted;
And beauty came like the setting sun:
My heart was shaken with tears; and horror
Drifted away . . . O, but Everyone
Was a bird; and the song was wordless; the singing will
never be done.

SIEGFRIED SASSOON

The Parable of the Old Man and the Young

So Abram rose, and clave the wood, and went,
And took the fire with him, and a knife.
And as they sojourned both of them together,
Isaac the first-born spake and said, My Father,
Behold the preparations, fire and iron,
But where the lamb for this burnt-offering?
Then Abram bound the youth with belts and straps,
And builded parapets and trenches there,
And stretchèd forth the knife to slay his son.
When lo! an angel called him out of heaven,
Saying, Lay not thy hand upon the lad,

Neither do anything to him. Behold,
A ram, caught in a thicket by its horns;
Offer the Ram of Pride instead of him.
But the old man would not so, but slew his son,
And half the seed of Europe, one by one.

WILFRED OWEN

Attack

At dawn the ridge emerges massed and dun
In the wild purple of the glow'ring sun,
Smouldering through spouts of drifting smoke that shroud
The menacing scarred slope; and, one by one,
Tanks creep and topple forward to the wire.
The barrage roars and lifts. Then, clumsily bowed
With bombs and guns and shovels and battle-gear,
Men jostle and climb to meet the bristling fire.
Lines of grey, muttering faces, masked with fear,
They leave their trenches, going over the top,   10
While time ticks blank and busy on their wrists,
And hope, with furtive eyes and grappling fists,
Flounders in mud. O Jesus, make it stop!

SIEGFRIED SASSOON

Break of Day in the Trenches

The darkness crumbles away –
It is the same old druid Time as ever.
Only a live thing leaps my hand –

A queer sardonic rat –
As I pull the parapet's poppy
To stick behind my ear.
Droll rat, they would shoot you if they knew
Your cosmopolitan sympathies.
Now you have touched this English hand
You will do the same to a German –
Soon, no doubt, if it be your pleasure
To cross the sleeping green between.
It seems you inwardly grin as you pass
Strong eyes, fine limbs, haughty athletes
Less chanced than you for life,
Bonds to the whims of murder,
Sprawled in the bowels of the earth,
The torn fields of France.
What do you see in our eyes
At the shrieking iron and flame
Hurled through still heavens?
What quaver – what heart aghast?
Poppies whose roots are in man's veins
Drop, and are ever dropping;
But mine in my ear is safe,
Just a little white with the dust.

ISAAC ROSENBERG

The Send-off

Down the close, darkening lanes they sang their way
To the siding-shed,
And lined the train with faces grimly gay.

Their breasts were stuck all white with wreath and spray
As men's are, dead.

Dull porters watched them, and a casual tramp
Stood staring hard,
Sorry to miss them from the upland camp.
Then, unmoved, signals nodded, and a lamp
Winked to the guard.   10

So secretly, like wrongs hushed-up, they went.
They were not ours:
We never heard to which front these were sent.
Nor there if they yet mock what women meant
Who gave them flowers.

Shall they return to beatings of great bells
In wild train-loads?
A few, a few, too few for drums and yells,
May creep back, silent, to village wells
Up half-known roads.   20

WILFRED OWEN

Spring Offensive

Halted against the shade of a last hill,
They fed, and lying easy, were at ease
And, finding comfortable chests and knees,
Carelessly slept. But many there stood still
To face the stark, blank sky beyond the ridge,
Knowing their feet had come to the end of the world.   75

Marvelling they stood, and watched the long grass swirled
By the May breeze, murmurous with wasp and midge,
For though the summer oozed into their veins
Like an injected drug for their bodies' pains,
Sharp on their souls hung the imminent line of grass,
Fearfully flashed the sky's mysterious glass.

Hour after hour they ponder the warm field –
And the far valley behind, where the buttercup
Had blessed with gold their slow boots coming up,
Where even the little brambles would not yield,
But clutched and clung to them like sorrowing hands;
They breathe like trees unstirred.

Till like a cold gust thrills the little word
At which each body and its soul begird
And tighten them for battle. No alarms
Of bugles, no high flags, no clamorous haste –
Only a lift and flare of eyes that faced
The sun, like a friend with whom their love is done.
O larger shone that smile against the sun, –
Mightier than his whose bounty these have spurned.

So, soon they topped the hill, and raced together
Over an open stretch of herb and heather
Exposed. And instantly the whole sky burned
With fury against them; earth set sudden cups
In thousands for their blood; and the green slope
Chasmed and steepened sheer to infinite space.

*   *   *

Of them who running on that last high place
Leapt to swift unseen bullets, or went up
On the hot blast and fury of hell's upsurge,
Or plunged and fell away past this world's verge,
Some say God caught them even before they fell.

But what say such as from existence' brink
Ventured but drave too swift to sink,
The few who rushed in the body to enter hell,   40
And there out-fiending all its fiends and flames
With superhuman inhumanities,
Long-famous glories, immemorial shames –
And crawling slowly back, have by degrees
Regained cool peaceful air in wonder –
Why speak not they of comrades that went under?

WILFRED OWEN

Gethsemane (1914–18)

The Garden called Gethsemane
    In Picardy it was,
And there the people came to see
    The English soldiers pass.

We used to pass – we used to pass
    Or halt, as it might be,
And ship our masks in case of gas
    Beyond Gethsemane.

The Garden called Gethsemane,
    It held a pretty lass,
But all the time she talked to me
    I prayed my cup might pass.
The officer sat on the chair,
    The men lay on the grass,
And all the time we halted there
    I prayed my cup might pass.

It didn't pass — it didn't pass —
    It didn't pass from me.
I drank it when we met the gas
    Beyond Gethsemane!

RUDYARD KIPLING

The Sentry

We'd found an old Boche dug out, and he knew,
And gave us hell; for shell on frantic shell
Lit full on top, but never quite burst through.
Rain, guttering down in waterfalls of slime,
Kept slush waist-high and rising hour by hour,
And choked the steps too thick with clay to climb.
What murk of air remained stank old, and sour
With fumes from whizbangs, and the smell of men
Who'd lived there years, and left their curse in the den,
If not their corpses . . .
                There we herded from the blast
Of whizbangs; but one found our door at last, —

Buffeting eyes and breath, snuffing the candles,
And thud! flump! thud! down the steep steps thumping
And sploshing in the flood, deluging muck,
The sentry's body; then his rifle, handles
Of old Boche bombs, and mud in ruck on ruck.
We dredged it up, for dead, until he whined
'O sir – my eyes, – I'm blind, – I'm blind, I'm blind.'
Coaxing, I held a flame against his lids
And said if he could see the least blurred light   20
He was not blind; in time they'd get all right.
'I can't,' he sobbed. Eyeballs, huge-bulged like squids
Watch my dreams still, – yet I forgot him there
In posting Next for duty, and sending a scout
To beg a stretcher somewhere, and floundring about
To other posts under the shrieking air.

Those other wretches, how they bled and spewed,
And one who would have drowned himself for good,
I try not to remember these things now.
Let Dread hark back for one word only: how,   30
Half-listening to that sentry's moans and jumps,
And the wild chattering of his shivered teeth,
Renewed most horribly whenever crumps
Pummelled the roof and slogged the air beneath,
Through the dense din, I say, we heard him shout
'I see your lights!' But ours had long gone out.

WILFRED OWEN

79

Futility

Move him into the sun –
Gently its touch awoke him once,
At home, whispering of fields unsown.
Always it woke him, even in France,
Until this morning and this snow.
If anything might rouse him now
The kind old sun will know.

Think how it wakes the seeds, –
Woke, once, the clays of a cold star.
Are limbs, so dear-achieved, are sides
Full-nerved, – still warm, – too hard to stir?
Was it for this the clay grew tall?
– O what made fatuous sunbeams toil
To break earth's sleep at all?

WILFRED OWEN

Dead Man's Dump

The plunging limbers over the shattered track
Racketed with their rusty freight,
Stuck out like many crowns of thorns,
And the rusty stakes like sceptres old
To stay the flood of brutish men
Upon our brothers dear.

The wheels lurched over sprawled dead
But pained them not, though their bones crunched,
Their shut mouths made no moan.
They lie there huddled, friend and foeman,   10
Man born of man, and born of woman,
And shells go crying over them
From night till night and now.

Earth has waited for them,
All the time of their growth
Fretting for their decay:
Now she has them at last!
In the strength of their strength
Suspended – stopped and held.

What fierce imaginings their dark souls lit?   20
Earth! have they gone into you!
Somewhere they must have gone,
And flung on your hard back
Is their soul's sack
Emptied of God-ancestralled essences.
Who hurled them out? Who hurled?

None saw their spirits' shadow shake the grass,
Or stood aside for the half used life to pass
Out of those doomed nostrils and the doomed mouth,
When the swift iron burning bee   30
Drained the wild honey of their youth.

What of us who, flung on the shrieking pyre,
Walk, our usual thoughts untouched,
Our lucky limbs as on ichor fed,   81

Immortal seeming ever?
Perhaps when the flames beat loud on us,
A fear may choke in our veins
And the startled blood may stop.

The air is loud with death,
The dark air spurts with fire,
The explosions ceaseless are.
Timelessly now, some minutes past,
These dead strode time with vigorous life,
Till the shrapnel called 'An end!'
But not to all. In bleeding pangs
Some borne on stretchers dreamed of home,
Dear things, war-blotted from their hearts.

Maniac Earth! howling and flying, your bowel
Seared by the jagged fire, the iron love,
The impetuous storm of savage love.
Dark Earth! dark Heavens! swinging in chemic smoke,
What dead are born when you kiss each soundless soul
With lightning and thunder from your mined heart,
Which man's self dug, and his blind fingers loosed?

A man's brains splattered on
A stretcher-bearer's face;
His shook shoulders slipped their load,
But when they bent to look again
The drowning soul was sunk too deep
For human tenderness.

They left this dead with the older dead,
Stretched at the cross roads.

40

50

60

82

Burnt black by strange decay
Their sinister faces lie,
The lid over each eye,
The grass and coloured clay
More motion have than they,
Joined to the great sunk silences.

Here is one not long dead;
His dark hearing caught our far wheels,   70
And the choked soul stretched weak hands
To reach the living word the far wheels said,
The blood–dazed intelligence beating for light,
Crying through the suspense of the far torturing wheels
Swift for the end to break
Or the wheels to break,
Cried as the tide of the world broke over his sight.

Will they come? Will they ever come?
Even as the mixed hoofs of the mules,
The quivering-bellied mules,   80
And the rushing wheels all mixed
With his tortured upturned sight.
So we crashed round the bend,
We heard his weak scream,
We heard his very last sound,
And our wheels grazed his dead face.

                                    ISAAC ROSENBERG

For the Fallen

(1914)

With proud thanksgiving, a mother for her children,
England mourns for her dead across the sea.
Flesh of her flesh they were, spirit of her spirit,
Fallen in the cause of the free.

Solemn the drums thrill: Death august and royal
Sings sorrow up into immortal spheres.
There is music in the midst of desolation
And a glory that shines upon our tears.

They went with songs to the battle, they were young,
Straight of limb, true of eye, steady and aglow.
They were staunch to the end against odds uncounted,
They fell with their faces to the foe.

They shall grow not old, as we that are left grow old:
Age shall not weary them, nor the years condemn.
At the going down of the sun and in the morning
We will remember them.

They mingle not with their laughing comrades again;
They sit no more at familiar tables of home;
They have no lot in our labour of the day-time;
They sleep beyond England's foam.

But where our desires are and our hopes profound,
Felt as a well-spring that is hidden from sight,

To the innermost heart of their own land they are known
As the stars are known to the Night;

As the stars that shall be bright when we are dust,
Moving in marches upon the heavenly plain,
As the stars that are starry in the time of our darkness,
To the end, to the end, they remain.

LAURENCE BINYON

The Rear-guard

(HINDENBURG LINE, APRIL 1917)

Groping along the tunnel, step by step,
He winked his prying torch with patching glare
From side to side, and sniffed the unwholesome air.

Tins, boxes, bottles, shapes too vague to know;
A mirror smashed, the mattress from a bed;
And he, exploring fifty feet below
The rosy gloom of battle overhead.

Tripping, he grabbed the wall; saw some one lie
Humped at his feet, half-hidden by a rug,
And stooped to give the sleeper's arm a tug.   10
'I'm looking for headquarters.' No reply.
'God blast your neck!' (For days he'd had no sleep,)
'Get up and guide me through this stinking place.'

Savage, he kicked a soft, unanswering heap,
And flashed his beam across the livid face
Terribly glaring up, whose eyes yet wore

85

Agony dying hard ten days before;
And fists of fingers clutched a blackening wound.

Alone he staggered on until he found
Dawn's ghost that filtered down a shafted stair
To the dazed, muttering creatures underground
Who hear the boom of shells in muffled sound.
At last, with sweat of horror in his hair,
He climbed through darkness to the twilight air,
Unloading hell behind him step by step.

SIEGFRIED SASSOON

Anthem for Doomed Youth

What passing-bells for these who die as cattle?
   Only the monstrous anger of the guns.
Only the stuttering rifles' rapid rattle
   Can patter out their hasty orisons.
No mockeries now for them; no prayers nor bells,
   Nor any voice of mourning save the choirs, –
The shrill, demented choirs of wailing shells;
   And bugles calling for them from sad shires.

What candles may be held to speed them all?
   Not in the hands of boys, but in their eyes
   Shall shine the holy glimmers of good-byes.
The pallor of girls' brows shall be their pall;
   Their flowers the tenderness of patient minds,
   And each slow dusk a drawing-down of blinds.

                                          WILFRED OWEN

Dulce et decorum est

Bent double, like old beggars under sacks,
Knock-kneed, coughing like hags, we cursed through
  sludge,
Till on the haunting flares we turned our backs,
And towards our distant rest began to trudge.
Men marched asleep. Many had lost their boots,
But limped on, blood-shod. All went lame, all blind;
Drunk with fatigue; deaf even to the hoots
Of gas-shells dropping softly behind.

Gas! GAS! Quick, boys! – An ecstasy of fumbling
Fitting the clumsy helmets just in time,   10
But someone still was yelling out and stumbling
And floundering like a man in fire or lime. –
Dim through the misty panes and thick green light
As under a green sea, I saw him drowning.

In all my dreams before my helpless sight
He plunges at me, guttering, choking, drowning.

If in some smothering dreams, you too could pace
Behind the wagon that we flung him in,
And watch the white eyes writhing in his face,
His hanging face, like a devil's sick of sin,   20
If you could hear, at every jolt, the blood
Come gargling from the froth-corrupted lungs
Bitter as the cud
Of vile, incurable sores on innocent tongues, –

My friend, you would not tell with such high zest
To children ardent for some desperate glory,
The old Lie: *Dulce et decorum est
Pro patria mori.*

WILFRED OWEN

Into Battle Flanders, April 1915

The naked earth is warm with Spring,
    And with green grass and bursting trees
Leans to the sun's gaze glorying,
    And quivers in the sunny breeze;

And life is colour and warmth and light,
    And a striving evermore for these;
And he is dead who will not fight;
    And who dies fighting has increase.

The fighting man shall from the sun
    Take warmth, and life from the glowing earth;
Speed with the light-foot winds to run,
    And with the trees to newer birth;
And find, when fighting shall be done,
    Great rest, and fullness after dearth.

All the bright company of Heaven
    Hold him in their high comradeship,
The Dog-Star, and the Sisters Seven,
    Orion's Belt and sworded hip.

The woodland trees that stand together,
    They stand to him each one a friend;

They gently speak in the windy weather;
    They guide to valley and ridge's end.

The kestrel hovering by day,
    And the little owls that call by night,
Bid him be swift and keen as they,
    As keen of ear, as swift of sight.

The blackbird sings to him, 'Brother, brother,
    If this be the last song you shall sing,
Sing well, for you may not sing another;
    Brother, sing.'   *30*

In dreary, doubtful waiting hours,
    Before the brazen frenzy starts,
The horses show him nobler powers;
    O patient eyes, courageous hearts!

And when the burning moment breaks,
    And all things else are out of mind,
And only joy of battle takes
    Him by the throat, and makes him blind,

Through joy and blindness he shall know,
    Not caring much to know, that still   *40*
Nor lead nor steel shall reach him, so
    That it be not the Destined Will.

The thundering line of battle stands,
    And in the air Death moans and sings;
But Day shall clasp him with strong hands,
    And Night shall fold him in soft wings.

JULIAN GRENFELL

The Dead

These hearts were woven of human joys and cares,
Washed marvellously with sorrow, swift to mirth.
The years had given them kindness. Dawn was theirs,
    And sunset, and the colours of the earth.
These had seen movement, and heard music; known
    Slumber and waking; loved; gone proudly friended;
Felt the quick stir of wonder; sat alone;
    Touched flowers and furs and cheeks. All this is ended.

There are waters blown by changing winds to laughter
And lit by the rich skies, all day. And after,
    Frost, with a gesture, stays the waves that dance
And wandering loveliness. He leaves a white
    Unbroken glory, a gathered radiance,
A width, a shining peace, under the night.

RUPERT BROOKE

From My Diary, July 1914

Leaves
    Murmuring by myriads in the shimmering trees.
Lives
    Wakening with wonder in the Pyrenees.
Birds
    Cheerily chirping in the early day.

Bards
   Singing of summer, scything thro' the hay.
Bees
   Shaking the heavy dews from bloom and frond.   *10*
Boys
   Bursting the surface of the ebony pond.
Flashes
   Of swimmers carving thro' the sparkling cold.
Fleshes
   Gleaming with wetness in the morning gold.
A mead
   Bordered about with warbling water brooks.
A maid
   Laughing the love-laugh with me; proud of looks.   *20*
The heat
   Throbbing between the upland and the peak.
Her heart
   Quivering with passion to my pressèd cheek.
Braiding
   Of floating flames across the mountain brow.
Brooding
   Of stillness; and a sighing of the bough.
Stirs
   Of leaflets in the gloom; soft petal-showers;   *30*
Stars
   Expanding with the starr'd nocturnal flowers.

WILFRED OWEN